Written by Elana K. Arnold

Illustrated by Elizabet Vuković

For Violet Becker, who arrived,
and Alex Kuczynski, who went away—E. K. A.

For Kiki—E. V.

BEACH LANE BOOKS
An imprint of Simon & Schuster Children's Publishing Division
1230 Avenue of the Americas, New York, New York 10020
Text copyright © 2020 by Elana K. Arnold
Illustrations copyright © 2020 by Elizabet Vuković
BEACH LANE BOOKS is a trademark of Simon & Schuster, Inc.
For information about special discounts for bulk purchases, please contact Simon & Schuster Special Sales
at 1-866-506-1949 or business@simonandschuster.com.
The Simon & Schuster Speakers Bureau can bring authors to your live event. For more information or to book an event,
contact the Simon & Schuster Speakers Bureau at 1-866-248-3049 or visit our website at www.simonspeakers.com.
Book design by Lauren Rille
The text for this book was set in Mrs. Eaves.
The illustrations for this book were rendered in charcoal, soft pastel, watercolor, ink, graphite and Adobe Photoshop.
Manufactured in China
1219 SCP
First Edition
10 9 8 7 6 5 4 3 2 1
Library of Congress Cataloging-in-Publication Data · Names: Arnold, Elana K., author. | Vuković, Elizabet, illustrator. · Title:
An ordinary day / Elana K. Arnold ; illustrated by Elizabet Vuković. · Description: First edition. | New York : Beach Lane Books,
[2020] | Summary: "An ordinary day in an ordinary neighborhood turns out to be extraordinary in this story about new life,
death, and family"—Provided by publisher. · Identifiers: LCCN 2018039905 | ISBN 9781481472623 (hardcover : alk. paper)
| ISBN 9781481472630 (eBook) · Subjects: | CYAC: Childbirth—Fiction. | Death—Fiction. | Family life—Fiction. | Neighbors—
Fiction. · Classification: LCC PZ7.A73517 Or 2020 | DDC [E]—dc23 LC record available at https://lccn.loc.gov/2018039905

An Ordinary Day

Beach Lane Books · New York London Toronto Sydney New Delhi

It was an ordinary day in the neighborhood.

There was Mrs. LaFleur, overwatering her roses.
There were Kia and Joseph, attempting to catch lizards.

There was Magnificent the Crow, letting everyone know that she saw what they were doing and that she did not approve.

Across the street, two houses sat unusually quiet.

Almost at the same time, a car pulled up to each.

From one car came a woman. She had a stethoscope draped around her neck, and she carried a little bag.

From the other car came a man.
Like the woman, he wore a stethoscope
around his neck, and he carried a little bag.

The visitors walked to the two front doors.

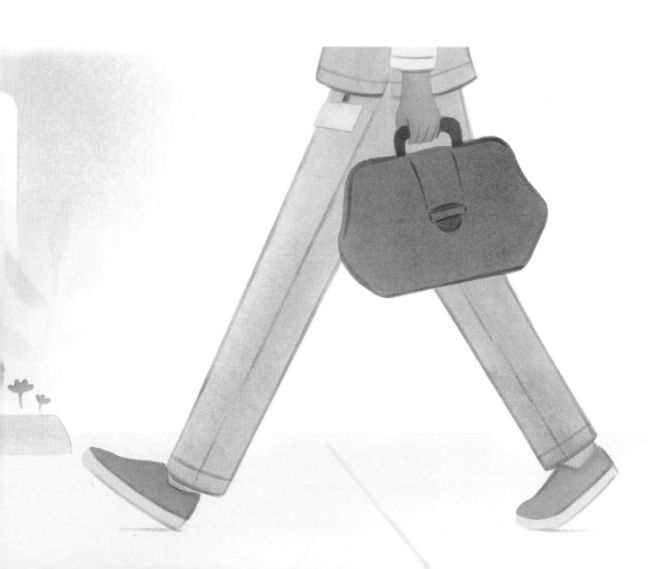

Each visitor raised a hand; each knocked quietly.

After a moment, each of the doors opened.

The two visitors slipped inside,
and once the doors closed, the street
seemed to forget about them entirely.

Inside the house on the left, a family gathered around a bed. On it lay the golden retriever named Sally. Music played, soft and without too many words.

Inside the house on the right, a woman rested on a bed.
Music played here too, soft and without too many words.

Each visitor unstrung a stethoscope.

Each visitor listened to a heartbeat.

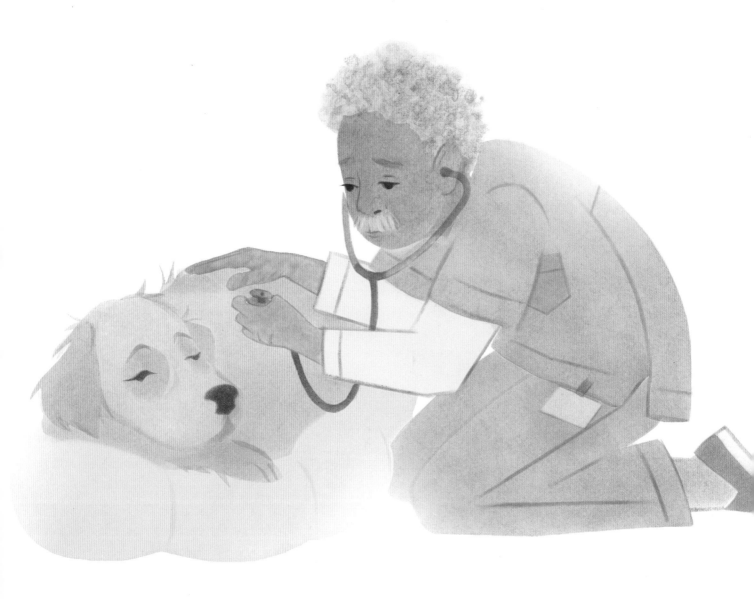

Each visitor looked up and spoke the same words:

"She is ready."

In the house on the left, the family prepared to say goodbye as the visitor filled a syringe of medicine.

In the house on the right, the family prepared to say hello as the visitor rubbed circles of oil into the woman's back.

Outside, Magnificent the Crow
continued her declarations
about everything.

The neighborhood children
went inside for ice pops. Mrs. LaFleur
turned off the spigot and wound the hose.

In the house on the left,
a final breath was exhaled,
surrounded by family and love.

And in the house on the right,
a first breath was inhaled,
surrounded by family and love.

For once, Magnificent the Crow fell silent.

A moment passed, a moment in which
the visitors,
the families,
the street,
and the world shifted.

It was an ordinary day in the neighborhood.
It was an extraordinary day in the neighborhood.

Like all days,
and all neighborhoods,
everywhere.